Unnatural Selections

WALLACE EDWARDS

ORCA BOOK PUBLISHERS

Library and Archives Canada Cataloguing in Publication

Edwards, Wallace, author
Unnatural selections / Wallace Edwards.

Issued in print and electronic formats.
ISBN 978-1-4598-0555-2 (BOUND).--ISBN 978-1-4598-0556-9 (PDF).--
ISBN 978-1-4598-0557-6 (EPUB)

I. Title.
PS8559.D88U55 2014   jc813'.6   c2014-901576-3   c2014-901577-1

First published in the United States, 2014
Library of Congress Control Number: 2014935386

Summary: A traveling artist takes the reader through a collection of illustrations of fantastical hybrid creatures.

Orca Book Publishers is dedicated to preserving the environment and has printed this book on Forest Stewardship Council® certified paper.

Orca Book Publishers gratefully acknowledges the support for its publishing programs provided by the following agencies: the Government of Canada through the Canada Book Fund and the Canada Council for the Arts, and the Province of British Columbia through the BC Arts Council and the Book Publishing Tax Credit.

Cover and interior artwork created using watercolor, gouache and pencil.

Cover artwork by Wallace Edwards
Design by Chantal Gabriell

ORCA BOOK PUBLISHERS
PO Box 5626, STN. B
Victoria, BC Canada
V8R 6S4

ORCA BOOK PUBLISHERS
PO Box 468
Custer, WA USA
98240-0468

www.orcabook.com
Printed and bound in Canada.

17 16 15 14 • 4 3 2 1

To Katie, my love, and to
Harriet, Stella, Gordon, George,
Sage and Chase.

—W.E.

Readers of this book, behold!

Beasts from an imagined age

Worlds where wondrous creatures roam

And come to life upon the page

Look close to find what's hidden in

This strange and lovely magic zoo

Full of creatures mixed and matched

Inspired by readers just like you!

———————◆———————

Professor I.B. Doodling, Traveling Artist

Whalephant

Whale + Elephant

Everyone who gets to see him,
secretly would like to be him.

Hawkodile

Hawk + Crocodile

She sits and ponders all the while,
the seldom-moving Hawkodile.

Toraffe

Tortoise + Giraffe

Her noble head held up with pride,
a balloon holds up her other side.

Cowaconda

Cow + Anaconda

See the lovely Cowaconda—
when her head is near, her body's yond-a.

Catfish

Cat + Fish

Though they share the same name,
no two are the same.

Rhimotherus

Rhino + Moth

His horn helps him know
where the sweet flowers grow.

Tyrabbosaurus Rex

T-rex + Rabbit

He loves when his tasty carrots
are delivered by friendly parrots.

Carpantelope
Carp + Panda + Antelope

With a swish of his tail,
he leaps over the rail.

Lizabouboon

Lizard + Caribou
+ Baboon

When his friends sing their song,
he plays along.

Leofroat

Leopard + Frog + Goat

Knowing spots look good on white,
the Leofroat's a handsome sight.

Shardunk
Shark + Duck + Skunk

The Shardunk's favorite trunks
have positively shrunk.

Skip

Moose + Pig + Swan + Zebra + Cheetah + Bat + Fox

A wondrous beast,
to say the least.

All these creatures are in this book.

Frunk

The fragrant type
of hopping stripe.

Mouzird

She lives in trees
and dreams of cheese.

Swox

The curious Swox
takes long walks.

Koalarus

His tusks of white
give him height.

Dorse

A dog and horse?
The Dorse of course.

Snailagator

Moving slow
way down below.

Zebraven

This creature moves
with beak and hooves.

Parram

A sight to see
perched on a tree.

Cameleon

While she's here,
she will disappear.

To find them, just take a look.

Ball-loon

He floats and flies
through cloudy skies.

Frogtopus

He wears no pants
and loves to dance.

Fishinch

It's no surprise
she swims and flies.

Girrat

Long neck and tail
and very pale.

Bumblebear

Inspecting things
with buzzing wings.

Eeleagle

He's very fond
of life in a pond.

Snird

Winding and sleek
with a beautiful beak.

Deerfly

A delicate thing
of antler and wing.

Horntoad

He toots a song
as he hops along.